The Musicians of Bremen

and other silly stories

Compiled by Vic Parker

Miles Kelly

First published in 2013 by Miles Kelly Publishing Ltd
Harding's Barn, Bardfield End Green, Thaxted, Essex, CM6 3PX, UK

This edition printed 2016

2 4 6 8 10 9 7 5 3

Publishing Director Belinda Gallagher
Creative Director Jo Cowan
Editorial Director Rosie Neave
Senior Editor Carly Blake
Editorial Assistant Amy Johnson
Designer Joe Jones
Production Elizabeth Collins, Caroline Kelly
Reprographics Stephan Davis, Jennifer Cozens, Thom Allaway
Assets Lorraine King

ISBN 978-1-84810-932-2

Printed in China

British Library Cataloguing-in-Publication Data
A catalogue record for this book is available from the British Library

ACKNOWLEDGMENTS
The publishers would like to thank the following artists who have contributed to this book:
Beehive Illustration Agency: Rosie Brooks, Mike Phillips (inc. cover)
The Bright Agency: Michael Garton
Aimee Mappley (decorative frames)

All other artwork from the Miles Kelly Artwork Bank

Made with paper from a sustainable forest

www.mileskelly.net

Contents

The Three Spinsters

By the Brothers Grimm

There was once a girl who was lazy and would not spin. No matter how her mother tried to persuade her to do it, she simply refused, point blank. At last the mother became angry and lost her patience, and she scolded the girl so much that she began to cry. At that moment the Queen was going by. As she heard the crying, she stopped. Going into the house, she asked the mother why she was scolding her daughter so that everyone outside in the street could hear her.

The woman was ashamed to tell of her daughter's laziness, so she said, "I cannot stop her from spinning. She is forever at it, and I am poor and cannot furnish her with enough flax."

The Queen was delighted and answered, "I like nothing better than the sound of the spinning-wheel, and always feel happy when I hear its humming. Let me take your daughter with me to the castle – I have plenty of flax. She shall spin there to her heart's content."

The mother was only too glad of the

chance to get rid of her lazy, unhelpful daughter, and the Queen took the girl with her.

When they reached the castle, the Queen showed the girl three rooms that were filled with the finest flax, as full as they could hold. "Now you can spin me this flax," said the Queen, "and when you can show it to me all done you shall have my eldest son for your bridegroom. You may be poor, but I make nothing of that – if you prove yourself to be as hardworking as your mother led me to believe, that will be good enough for me."

The girl was inwardly terrified, for she could not have spun the flax even if she were to live to be a hundred years old, and

were to sit spinning every day of her life
from morning to evening. When she found
herself alone she began to weep, and sat so
for three days without putting her hand to
the spinning-wheel.

On the third day the Queen came, and
when she saw that nothing had been done

of the spinning she was much surprised. The girl excused herself by saying that she had not been able to begin because of the distress she was in at leaving her home and her mother. The excuse contented the Queen, who said, as she went away, "Tomorrow you must begin to work."

When the girl found herself alone again she could not tell how to help herself or what to do, and in her upset she went and gazed out of the window. There she saw three women passing by. The first of them had a broad flat foot, the second had a big under-lip that hung down over her chin, and the third had a remarkably broad thumb. They all of them stopped in front of the window, and called out to know what it was that the girl wanted. She told them about the awful situation she found herself in. The girl couldn't believe her ears when the three ugly women promised her their help, and said, "Then will you invite us to your wedding, and not be ashamed of us, and call us your cousins, and let us sit at your table? If you will promise this, we will finish off your flax-spinning in a very short time."

"With all my heart," answered the girl, "only come in now, and begin at once." Of course, she would have promised them anything at all to have the spinning done in time to show the Queen!

Then these same women came in, and she cleared a space in the first room for

them to sit and begin their spinning. The
first one drew out the thread and moved the
treddle that turned the wheel. The second
moistened the thread. The third twisted it
and rapped with her finger on the table,
and as often as she rapped, a heap of yarn
fell to the ground, and it was most
beautifully spun.

The girl hid the three spinsters out of the
Queen's sight, and only showed her, as often
as she came, the heaps of well-spun yarn.
There was no end to the praises she
received. When the first room was empty
the women went on to the second, and then
to the third, so that at last all of the flax had
been spun.

Then the three women took their leave,

saying to the girl, "Do not forget what you have promised and it will be all the better for you."

So when the girl took the Queen and showed her the empty rooms and the great heaps of yarn, the wedding was at once arranged. The bridegroom rejoiced that he should have so clever and hardworking a wife, and praised her exceedingly.

"I have three cousins," said the girl, "and as they have shown me a great deal of kindness, I would not wish to forget them in my good fortune. May I be allowed to invite them to the wedding, and to ask them to sit at the table with us?"

The Queen and the bridegroom said at once, "Of course."

The Three Spinsters

So when the feast began, in came the three spinsters in strange guise, and the bride said, "Dear cousins, you are welcome."

"Oh," said the bridegroom, "how did you come to have such dreadfully ugly relations?" Then he went up to the first spinster and said, "How is it that you have such a broad flat foot?"

"With treading," answered she, "with treading."

Then he went up to the second and said, "How is it that you have such a great hanging lip?"

"With licking," answered she, "with licking."

Then he asked the third, "How is it that you have such a broad thumb?"

"With twisting thread," answered she,

13

"with twisting thread."

Then the bridegroom said that from that time forward his beautiful bride should never touch a spinning-wheel.

And so she escaped that tiresome flax-spinning once and for all.

The Stone Soup

A folk tale

Many years ago three soldiers were on their way home from war, hungry and weary of battle, when they came upon a small village. The villagers had suffered a poor harvest because so many of them had been called away to fight. They quickly hid what little food they had and met the three strangers in the village square, moaning about how starving they all were.

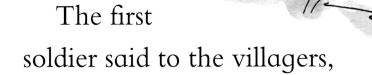

The first
soldier said to the villagers,
"Your tired fields have left you nothing
to share. We will share what little we have –
the secret of how to make soup from stones."

A murmur of excitement rippled through
the crowd. Soon a fire was put to the town's
greatest pot. Everyone watched with
curiosity as the soldiers dropped in three
stones. "Now this will be a fine soup," said

the second soldier, "but a pinch of salt and some parsley would make it wonderful!"

Up jumped a villager, crying, "I've just remembered where some is!"

She returned with an apronful of parsley and a turnip to boot.

The memory of the villagers strangely seemed to improve. Soon barley, carrots, beef and cream had found their way into the great pot, and even a barrel of wine was rolled into the square.

It didn't seem long before everyone was sitting down to a delicious-smelling, rich soup, packed with tasty, chunky vegetables.

The villagers ate and danced and sang well into the night, refreshed by the feast and their new-found friends. They couldn't remember when they had last had such an enjoyable meal. It was the early hours of the morning before everyone finally turned in to bed.

When the three soldiers awoke they found the entire village standing before them. At their feet lay a satchel of the village's best breads and cheese. "You have given us the greatest of gifts – the secret of

how to make soup from stones," said an elder, "and we shall never forget."

The third soldier turned to the crowd, and said, "There is no secret, but this is certain – it is only by sharing that we may make a feast."

And off the soldiers wandered down the road, leaving the villagers bewildered but thoughtful behind them.

The Greedy Brownie

Edited by Hamilton Wright Mabie,
Edward Everett Hale and
William Byron Forbush

There was once a little Brownie who lived in a hollow tree stump. He had been busy all the day playing pranks, as all Brownies love to do. His pranks had taken him far away from home to the house of a very important landowner. Into the landowner's cup of wine the Brownie had dropped some horribly sour berries, which he had picked on his way. The Brownie also put prickly thistles into the landowner's boots, so that when he had drawn them on he had screamed out with pain.

The Brownie had been away all the day, so when at last he turned to go back to his home he felt really very tired. On his way back to the wood he passed by a cozy-looking farmhouse, and the door of the dairy was open. The Brownie thought this would be a very nice cool place in which to rest for a few moments. So he slipped into the dairy and curled himself up underneath the bench to have a nice little doze.

He was so weary that once he had fallen asleep he never woke up again until it was quite dark. He was disturbed by two young

The Greedy Brownie

girls who had come into the dairy. One was carrying a candle, and by its light the pair spied a big bowl of cream on the shelf. The naughty girls thought that they would drink it for supper. They could only find one spoon on the shelf, so they decided they would each have a spoonful in turn.

One of the girls, Jean, carried the bowl to a bench in the corner, and the other, Meg, followed with the candle. No sooner had the two girls settled themselves than the Brownie, who was now wide awake and feeling that some supper might not be out of place, crept up behind them and blew out the candle.

The girls at first were very concerned at being in the dark. Nevertheless, they determined they would drink the cream all the same. Jean filled the spoon with the rich delicacy. She was about to raise it to her lips when the naughty Brownie poked his head over her shoulder, and lapped it out of the spoon before it had reached her mouth.

Meg, believing that Jean had already swallowed some cream while she had had none, stretched out her hand to take away the spoon from her friend. Jean was not willing to give it up, since she said she had not yet tasted any cream.

Meg was unwilling to believe her, for she declared she had heard her lapping the cream. Without waiting for Jean to explain, she snatched the spoon from her friend's hand. She filled it with cream from the bowl, and was about to raise it to her lips when the Brownie jumped from behind Jean, and settled himself behind the shoulders of Meg. He poked forward his head, and again lapped up the cream from out of the spoon. Jean, in her turn, snatched

back the spoon from Meg…

And so they went on, for every time one or the other raised the spoonful of cream to her lips it was lapped up by the gleeful Brownie. This continued until the bowl was completely emptied. The Brownie was full of cream and quite drunk with happiness, but the young girls had not tasted one drop, although each believed the other had drunk it all.

The foolish girls were still arguing when the door of the dairy was opened, and the farmer's wife entered, carrying a lighted candle in her hand. The moment that she did so the mischievous Brownie hopped underneath the bench, and the girls started up guiltily.

At once, the farmer's wife caught sight of the empty bowl. She was very angry with the two girls indeed. When they tried hastily to explain, each blaming the other, the farmer's wife would not listen, but only grew more angry. She told them that, since they had supped so well, they should have none of the scones and eggs which she had prepared for the evening meal.

When the farmer's wife had entered she had left the door open, so while she was busily scolding the girls the naughty Brownie slipped out from under the bench and made his escape. As he ran chuckling down the road, he could still hear the farmer's wife's angry voice drowning the explanations of the bewildered girls.

When the little fellow curled himself up some time later in his hollow tree stump he was still laughing.

The Musicians of Bremen

By the Brothers Grimm

An honest farmer once had an donkey
that had been a faithful servant to him for a
great many years. But the donkey was now
growing old and every day more and more
unfit for work. His master therefore was
tired of keeping him and began to think of
getting rid of him. The donkey, who saw

that some mischief was in the wind, took himself slyly off, and began his journey toward the town of Bremen. 'For there,' he thought, 'I may become a musician and make my fortune that way.'

After he had wandered a little way, he spied a dog lying by the roadside, panting as if he were tired. "What makes you pant so, my friend?" said the donkey.

"Alas," said the dog, "my master was going to knock me on the head because I am old and weak and can no longer make myself useful to him in hunting, so I ran away. What can I do to earn my living?"

"Listen to this," said the donkey, "I am going to Bremen to become a musician. Suppose you come with me, and try what you can do in the same way?"

The dog said he was willing, and they jogged on together.

They had not gone far before they saw a cat sitting in the middle of the road, looking most downcast. "Hello there, my good lady," said the donkey, "what's the matter with you? You look quite out of spirits!"

"Ah, me!" said the cat. "How can one be in good spirits when one's life is in danger? Because I am beginning to grow old, and had rather lie at my ease by the fire than run about the house after mice, my mistress caught me by the scruff of the neck and was going to drown me. Though I have been lucky enough to get away from her, I do not know what is to become of me."

"Oh," said the donkey, "by all means come with us to Bremen. You are a good night singer and may make your fortune as a musician."

The cat was pleased with the thought, and joined the party.

Soon afterward, as they were passing by a farmyard, they saw a rooster perched upon a gate, screaming out with all his might and main.

"Bravo!" said the donkey. "Upon my word, you make a famous noise. Pray, what is all this about?"

"Why," said the rooster, "I was just now saying that we should have fine weather for our washing day. Yet my mistress and the cook don't thank me for my pains, but threaten to cut off my head tomorrow, and make broth of me for the guests that are coming on Sunday!"

"Heaven forbid!" said the donkey. "Come with us, Master Rooster. It will be better, at any rate, than staying here to have your head cut off! Besides, who knows? If we sing in tune, we may get up some kind of a concert, so come along with us."

"With all my heart," said the rooster, so they all four went on happily together.

They could not, however, reach the town the first day. So when night came on, they went into a wood to sleep. The donkey and the dog laid themselves down under a great tree, and the cat climbed up into the branches. The rooster, thinking that the higher he sat the safer he should be, flew up to the very top of the tree and then, as usual, before he went to sleep, looked out on all sides of him to see that everything was well. In doing this, he saw far off something bright and shining, and calling to his companions said, "There must be a house nearby, for I see a light."

"If that be the case," said the donkey, "let

us go and see if we can stay there, for our current arrangement is hardly the best in the world!"

"Besides," added the dog, "I should not be the worse for a bone or two, or a nice bit of meat."

So they walked off together toward the spot where the rooster had seen the light. As they drew near the light, it became larger, till they at last came close to a house.

Little did the unfortunate band of animals know that it was a house in which a gang of robbers lived.

The donkey, being the tallest of the company, marched up to the window and peeped in. "Well, Donkey," said the rooster, "what do you see?"

"What do I see?" replied the donkey. "Why, I see a table spread with all kinds of good things, and robbers sitting round it making merry."

"That would be a perfect lodging place for us," said the rooster.

"Yes," said the donkey, "if we could only get in." So they put their heads together and thought hard about how they might be able to get the robbers out, and at last they hit upon a plan.

The donkey placed himself upright on his hind legs, with his forefeet resting against the window. The dog got upon his back, the cat scrambled up to the dog's shoulders, and the rooster flew up and sat upon the cat's head. When all was ready a

signal was given, and they began their music. The donkey brayed, the dog barked, the cat mewed, and the rooster screamed. Then they all broke through the window at once, and came tumbling into the room, amongst the broken glass, with a most hideous clatter!

The robbers, who had been not a little frightened by the opening concert, had now no doubt that some frightful hobgoblin had broken in upon them, and scampered away as fast as it could.

Once the coast was clear, our animals sat down and gobbled up what the robbers had left with eagerness. As soon as they had satisfied themselves, they put out the lights, and each once more sought out a resting place to his own liking. The donkey laid himself down upon a heap of straw in the yard, the dog stretched himself upon a mat behind the door, the cat curled up on the hearth before the warm ashes, and the rooster perched upon a beam on the top of the house. They were all tired with their journey, and soon fell asleep.

About midnight, when the robbers saw from afar that the lights were out and all seemed quiet, they began to think that they had been in too great a hurry to run away. One of them went to see what was going on. Finding everything still, he marched into the kitchen and groped about till he found a match to light a candle. Then, spying the glittering fiery eyes of the cat, he mistook them for live coals, and held the match to them to light it. The cat, not understanding this joke, sprang at his face and scratched at him. This frightened the robber, and away he ran to the back door. There the dog jumped up and bit him on the leg, and as he was crossing over the yard the donkey kicked him, and the rooster, who had been awakened by the noise, crowed with all his might. At this the robber ran back as fast as he could to his comrades, and told the captain how a horrid witch had got into the house, and had spat at him and scratched his face with her long bony fingers, how a man with a knife in his hand had hidden himself behind the door and stabbed him in the leg, how a black monster stood in the yard and struck him with a club, and how the devil had sat upon the top of the house and cried, "Throw the rascal up here!"

After this the robbers never dared to go back to the house. The musicians were so pleased with their quarters that they took up their home there, and there they are, I dare say, to this very day.